characters created by lauren child

I can't STOP hiccuping!

Grosset & Dunlap
An Imprint of Penguin Group (USA) Inc.

Text based on
the script written by
David Ingham

Illustrations from
the TV animations
produced by
Tiger Aspect

GROSSET & DUNLAP
Published by the Penguin Group
Penguin Group (USA) Inc., 375 Hudson Street, New York, New York 10014, USA
Penguin Group (Canada), 90 Eglinton Avenue East, Suite 700, Toronto, Ontario M4P 2Y3, Canada
(a division of Pearson Penguin Canada Inc.)
Penguin Books Ltd., 80 Strand, London WC2R 0RL, England
Penguin Group Ireland, 25 St. Stephen's Green, Dublin 2, Ireland
(a division of Penguin Books Ltd.)
Penguin Group (Australia), 250 Camberwell Road, Camberwell, Victoria 3124, Australia
(a division of Pearson Australia Group Pty. Ltd.)
Penguin Books India Pvt. Ltd., 11 Community Centre, Panchsheel Park, New Delhi—110 017, India
Penguin Group (NZ), 67 Apollo Drive, Rosedale, North Shore 0632, New Zealand
(a division of Pearson New Zealand Ltd.)
Penguin Books (South Africa) (Pty.) Ltd., 24 Sturdee Avenue,
Rosebank, Johannesburg 2196, South Africa

Penguin Books Ltd., Registered Offices: 80 Strand, London WC2R 0RL, England

Published by Grosset & Dunlap, a division of Penguin Young Readers Group, 345 Hudson Street,
New York, New York 10014. GROSSET & DUNLAP is a trademark of Penguin Group (USA) Inc. Manufactured in China.

Library of Congress Cataloging-in-Publication Data is available.

ISBN 978-0-448-45329-3

10 9 8 7 6 5 4 3 2 1

I have this little sister, Lola.
She is small and very funny.
Lola is practicing the words to her song.
She is **singing** it with Lotta tonight
at the school **concert**.

Lola and Lotta sing,

The spring is here,
the cold has fled.
The flowers bloom
and raise their heads.

Spring is here!
Spring is here!
Spring is here at last!

Then Lola and Lotta
giggle . . .
and giggle . . .
until—*HIC!*—
Lola hiccups!

At recess Lola says,
"My hiccups won't—*HIC!*—
go away!"

So I say, "I have an idea.
Look at my finger
very, very closely."

Then Marv jumps
out of nowhere.
"BOO!"

Lola screams.
"Why did you do that?"

Marv says,
"To scare away your hiccups."

And Lola says,
"They're completely gone!"

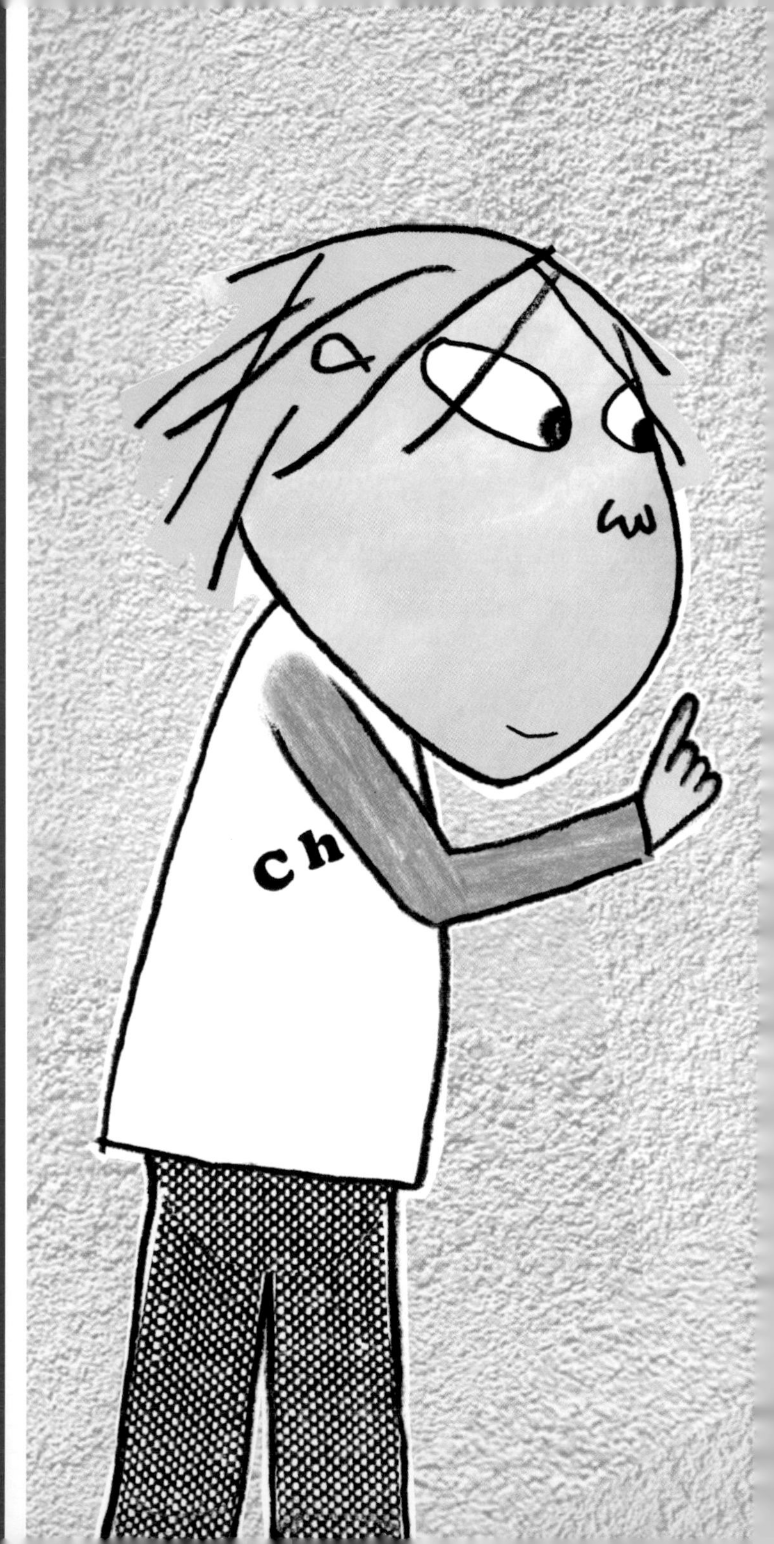

In art class,
Lola paints a bird
with a big tail
and a teeny, tiny beak.

HIC!

When Lola **hiccups**,
her brush flies
across the painting.

Arnold says,
"Now it looks like
an airplane."

Lola says,
"But I didn't want to—
HIC!—paint an airplane."

In class Lola says,
"The concert's going to be
all right now that
my hiccups have
gone away."

Lotta says, "Oh yes.
Do you like my tower?"

Lola leans in
for a closer look.
HIC!

Lola knocks
Lotta's tower over.

Lola says,
"Sorry—*HIC!*—Lotta!"

At lunch, everyone tells Lola different ways to get rid of her hiccups.

She pats her head and rubs her tummy.

She drinks from the wrong side of her cup.

She says, “AAHHH!”
for as long as she can.

Then Lola tries lying
on her back and wiggling
her legs in the air.

Lotta asks,
“Is it working?”

And Lola says,
“Yes! They’re gone!”

But later,
during our snack . . .
HIC!
Lola's hiccups come back.

"Ohhh . . ."
Lola says.
"At first, they were funny.
But I don't want
to have them
ANYMORE."

I say,
"Sometimes things
can be fun at first,
but then you can get
a bit fed up.
Like strawberries.
The first one's always
super delicious."

And Lola says,
"But if you
eat too many of them,
they are not fun.
Just like my hiccups."

So I say,
"What hiccups?"

And Lola says,
"They're gone again!"

Lola and Lotta
are backstage
before the school concert.

Lola says,
"I haven't hiccuped
for nearly
one whole hour."

Lotta says,
"Should we have
one last little practice?"

Lola and Lotta sing
their song, and they
giggle and giggle.
Then, *HIC!*

Lola says,
"Oh no! *HIC!*
We'd better get Charlie."

Lola says,
"Lotta made me—*HIC!*—
laugh, and I got
the hiccups again.
How can I—*HIC!*—sing
with the hiccups?"

So I say,
"Try making ME laugh
so I can catch your hiccups.
Then you won't
have them!"

Lola wiggles and
makes silly faces.
Lotta blows a raspberry.

I say,
"Hee hee hee . . . *HIC!*"

Onstage, Lotta and Lola
sing their song.

The spring is here,
the cold has fled.
The flowers bloom
and raise their heads.

Spring is here!
Spring is here!
Spring is here at last!

Lola sings the song
without even
one little hiccup!
Everyone claps,
especially me and Marv.

Marv asks, "How did you do it?"

I say, "I pretended Lola had given her **hiccups** to me."

We laugh, and all of a sudden I . . . *HIC!*

Marv says, "Very funny, Charlie."

I say, "*HIC!* Now I really have the **hiccups**!"